To.....................
.....
From................
.....

With Love

A Celebration of Words
and Pictures for the
Very Young

About Wendy Cooling

Wendy Cooling taught English in London schools for twenty years before moving to head up the children's side of Booktrust, a charity working to promote reading. There she set up Bookstart, which aims to encourage parents and carers to read to their babies when they are very young. Wendy is now recognised as a children's book guru – she regularly speaks on radio and television and travels the world to talk about children's books. She has talked about books and reading all around the UK as well as in the US and Malaysia – and has helped to launch Bookstart in Thailand and Korea. She loves to travel and has cycled round China, walked in the Himalayas and the Andes, and she continues to journey everywhere she can! She lives in London and loves the theatre and the music it offers – and, of course, she reads and reads and reads . . .

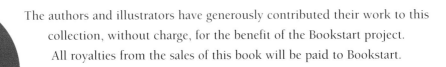

The authors and illustrators have generously contributed their work to this collection, without charge, for the benefit of the Bookstart project.
All royalties from the sales of this book will be paid to Bookstart.

ORCHARD BOOKS
96 Leonard Street, London EC2A 4XD
Orchard Books Australia
32/45-51 Huntley Street, Alexandria, NSW 2015
ISBN 1 84362 414 1
First published in Great Britain in 2004
Compilation © Wendy Cooling 2004
Text and illustrations © the individual authors and illustrators credited 2004
Elmer™ © David McKee
The moral rights of Wendy Cooling and the authors and illustrators of this compilation have been asserted by them in accordance with the Copyright, Designs and Patents Act, 1988.
A CIP catalogue record for this book is available from the British Library.
2 4 6 8 10 9 7 5 3 1
Printed in Hong Kong, China, by the South China Printing Company Limited, who have kindly supported Bookstart.

Book character publisher details:
'Duck' by Jez Alborough (HarperCollins)
'Chimp and Zee' by Catherine and Laurence Anholt (Frances Lincoln)
'Lily and Blue Kangaroo' by Emma Chichester Clark (Andersen Press)
'Flora' by Debi Gliori (Orchard Books)
'Elmer' by David McKee (Andersen Press)
'Baby Bear' by John Prater (Random House)

With Love

A Celebration of Words and Pictures
for the Very Young

Compiled by Wendy Cooling

ORCHARD BOOKS

Contents

Additional artwork by Annie Kubler, Neal Layton,
Helen Oxenbury and Arthur Robins.

Foreword

Wendy Cooling, illustrated by Tony Ross

 *I THINK I WAS BORN WITH A PASSION FOR BOOKS* and I've been lucky enough to spend my working life sharing this with children – and adults too! So it's been a joy to put together this collection in celebration of Bookstart – a project that offers two beautiful books as a gift to all babies in the UK at their eight-month health check. Do read more about Bookstart at the back of this book. This collection introduces families to the very best authors and illustrators of today – and reflects my belief that a book can be shared with a baby right from the start. I want this whole book to speak to children, so here are a few lines about reading that can be shared with them:

Take any page,
read at any time.
Listen to the words speak,
to their rhythm and their rhyme.

Look at the pictures,
point to them too,
their colours and their characters
are all there for you.

Read stories over and over,
they're so good to share.
Tiny children will listen
they'll look and they'll stare.

*Children will giggle,
they'll interrupt and they'll chatter.
Join in with their fun,
noise just doesn't matter.*

*Reading is for pleasure,
for fun – just like play.
Read these rhymes, poems and stories
till the end of the day.*

My thanks of course go to all the wonderful authors and illustrators who have contributed so generously and creatively to this book – they are all to be celebrated along with all children and the Bookstart project.

With love

Wendy Cooling

I'm Going on a Train!

Sally Grindley, illustrated by Lindsey Gardiner

I'm going on a train!

I'm waiting at the station because
I'm going on a train!

The signal's turned to green.
The train must be coming because
the signal's turned to green.

I can see a cloud of smoke.
I can hear a loud whistle.
There's another cloud of smoke and
the noise is getting louder and . . .

14

It's the train! It's the train!

The train is in the station and
I'm waving to the driver.
The train is in the station and
I'm climbing up on board.
The guard has blown his whistle and
I'm sitting by the window.
The guard has blown his whistle and

we're off!

DUCK in the TRUCK

Jez Alborough

This is the duck
who waves from his truck.

This is the sheep
who arrives in his jeep.

This is the frog
who jumps up
from his log.

This is the goat who cries:
"Climb on my boat."

And this is the fun they all have in the sun.

ROUND AND ROUND the JUNGLE
Catherine and Laurence Anholt

Once upon a time in a coconut tree
Lived two small monkeys named Chimp and Zee

They climbed down the ladder, one, two, three!
Round and round the jungle - hee, hee, hee!

"Now then," says Mumkey, "Let me see,
Once upon a time in a coconut tree . . ."

And jumped right up on the big settee
For story time on Mumkey's knee

RO-OO-AR!

Chimp chased a butterfly, Zee chased a bee
And they tugged something hairy – what could it be?

BOO, HOO, HOO! WEE, WEE, WEE!
Oh, please Mr Lion, don't eat me!

You can't have monkeys for your tea
Bananas are best, don't you agree?

Then they ran back home as fast as can be
Climbed up the ladder, one, two, three!

Monster Dad

Chris Riddell

When I hear a bump in the night
or a creak on the stair,
I'm never afraid . . .
because my dad is there!

Lily and Blue Kangaroo at the Zoo

Emma Chichester Clark

Lily and Blue Kangaroo
spent the day with their friends
at the zoo.

The monkeys were naughty
the lions were haughty,

but a parrot said,
"How do you do?"

How do you do?

When Lily lost Blue Kangaroo
she caused a great hullabaloo!

Everyone hurried,
they needn't have worried . . .

. . . he popped up and said,

"Peekaboo!"

My Mummy

Giles Andreae,
illustrated by Adrian Reynolds

I love my mummy madly
She always makes me laugh
I sing and clap and dance with her
And giggle in the bath

She wipes my grubby nosey
And she sucks my smelly feet
And even when I cry a lot
She says I'm very sweet

But my favourite thing about her
When we're cuddled up in bed
Is to squish my little nappy
Up against her sleeping head

Doing the Best I Can

Adrian Mitchell, illustrated by Clara Vulliamy

*Dad
showed me
my new
half-sister.*

*I love Dad
so I
half-kissed her.*

Breakfast in Bed

Jeremy Strong, illustrated by Guy Parker-Rees

It was half-past five in the morning. Small Hippo was wide awake. He jumped out of bed and did his morning exercises.

"Did you hear a noise?" mumbled Mr Hippo.
"I heard you snoring," grumbled Mrs Hippo.
"Go back to sleep, you big lump."
"Big lump yourself," grunted Mr Hippo fondly.

Small Hippo crept downstairs. He buttered some bread. He put cornflakes and tomato sauce on top.

Lovely!

26

What next? Aha! Breakfast in bed
for Mummy and Daddy!
He needed eggs and milk . . . **Splurrrp!**

Small Hippo
took out the mop.

"Whoops! Ouch!"

"Uh?" grunted Mr Hippo.
"Did I hear a crash in the kitchen?"
"You're dreaming, you big bumbling bulldozer."
"I'll go and have a look," sighed Mr Hippo.

Small Hippo tried to clean up.
Mr Hippo opened the kitchen door.
"What is all this,
Small Hippo?"

"I'm making breakfast in bed for you and Mummy,"
sniffed Small Hippo.

"Breakfast in bed!" smiled Mr Hippo. "I can
see breakfast on the floor and breakfast
on the walls, but luckily you've
missed the beds, so far."

Small Hippo burst into tears.
Mr Hippo kissed his sticky face.
"Never mind, no harm done.
Let's clean up together."

Small Hippo was very tired so Mr Hippo made
the special breakfast instead.

"Let's take breakfast up to Mummy."

"What a lovely surprise!" said Mrs Hippo.

And they all squeezed into Mr and Mrs Hippo's bed.

"This is brilliant!" said Small Hippo.

But . . .

KERRRUNCH!

Mr Hippo grinned.

"Breakfast in bed,"

he announced!

Flora's Blanket

Debi Gliori

How I love my blanket.

I use it as a tent.

I sail it like a boat.

I fly with blanket wings.

You can't see me under my disappearing blanket.

Eeek! It's a blanket ghost!

Best of all, I love my blanket of dreams.

The Happy Nappy Rhyme

Sarah Garland

Down you go,

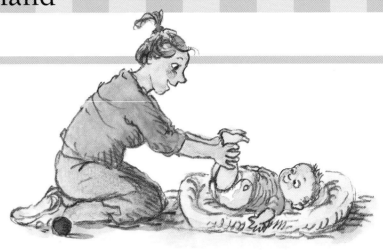

look at your toes,

Up you come,

with a dum-di-dum . . .

Hush-a-bye,

Pat you dry,

off with your nappy

and KISS on your nose.

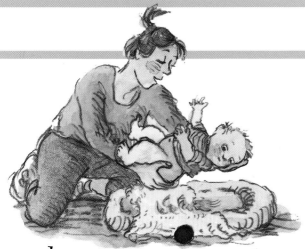

clean as a whistle

and BLOW on your tum.

on with your nappy

and FLY in the sky.

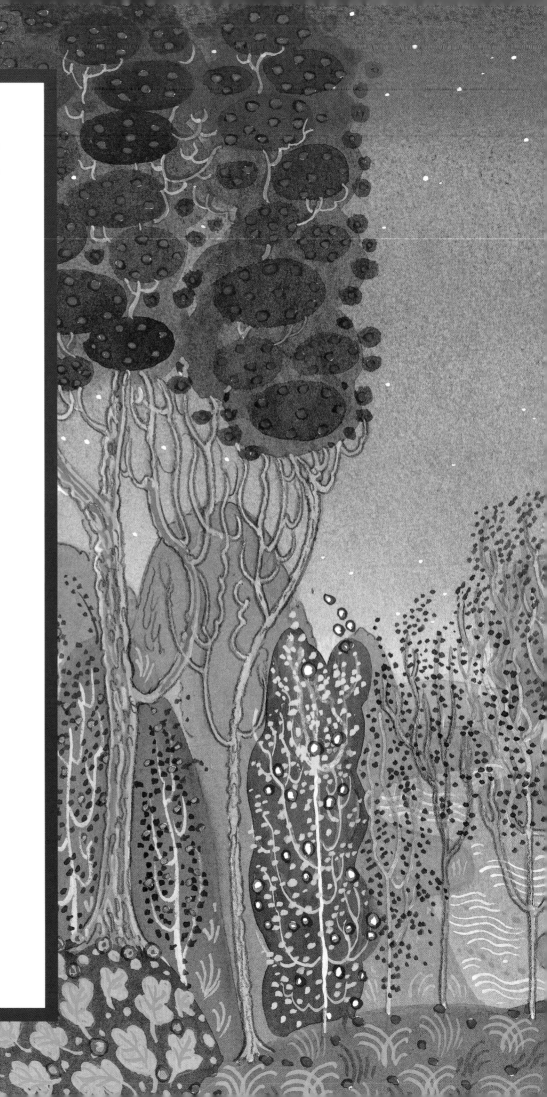

Moon Song

Ian Beck

In the night
I love to see
The Moon as it
Smiles down at me

In the night
I love to see
The stars that
Shine so bright to me

In the night
I love to see
My Mother's face,
She bends to kiss
Goodnight to me.

Bernard's Buttons

Martin Waddell, illustrated by Paul Howard

Bernard had a new coat,
but he didn't know how to do up the buttons.

Bernard buttoned his first button up,
but it didn't look right,
so Bernard unbuttoned his button.

Bernard tried the next button,
but it didn't look right,
so Bernard unbuttoned his button.

Bernard tried the last button,
but it didn't look right,
so Bernard unbuttoned his button.

"Bother these buttons!" said Bernard.

"Line the buttons up beside each
buttonhole," Max told Bernard.

Bernard buttoned the top button up,
in the top buttonhole.
It looked good.

Bernard buttoned the next button up,
in the next buttonhole.
It looked good too.

Bernard buttoned the last button up,
in the last buttonhole.
It looked R-I-G-H-T!

And that's how Bernard
buttoned his buttons.

Elmer

David McKee

Elmer is yellow and orange too.
Elmer is red, pink, purple and blue.
Elmer is green and black and white,
a patchwork elephant, very bright.

Me, Me, Me

Benjamin Zephaniah,
illustrated by Jan Ormerod

Eyes and nose and ears and lips
Bits of hair and fingertips,
Heels and toes on little feet
And a mouth to help you eat.

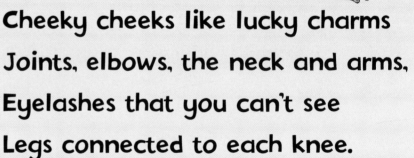

Cheeky cheeks like lucky charms
Joints, elbows, the neck and arms,
Eyelashes that you can't see
Legs connected to each knee.

We must not forget the chin
And those bits that are within,
Parts that must not be forgotten
Like the belly and the bottom.

My Cat

Wendy Cooling, illustrated by James Mayhew

An elephant is huge
A mouse is small
Some dogs are short
All giraffes are tall.

Snakes slither silently
Monkeys chatter and call
My cat purrs quietly
I love her best of all.

Stomp! Stomp!

Jeanne Willis, illustrated by Tony Ross

Knock! Knock!

Who's there?
A mini monster!

Stomp! Stomp!

Here he comes
Down the hall.

Crash! Bash!

What's he doing
In our kitchen?

Clanging pans
Bashing tins
Smashing plates

He's looking
For something
But it's not there!

42

Stomp! Stomp!

Off he goes
To the playroom.

Blowing trumpets
Booting footballs
Tooting hooters

He's looking
For something
But it's not there!

Stomp! Stomp!

Off he goes
To the bathroom.

Squishing soap
Flinging flannels
Poking plugholes

He's looking
For something
But it's not there!

Stomp! Stomp!
Off he goes
To Baby's room.

Monster stops.
Monster stares,
"It's there! It's there!"

"That's **my** teddy!
Not yours!"
roars Monster.

Stomp! Stomp!
Off he goes
Home to Mummy.

I Love Ketchup!

Giles Andreae, illustrated by Korky Paul

I love ketchup
I love it just to bits
But my mummy says it's only good
With dippy things like chips
So when she isn't looking
I grab it and I squeeze
And oops! It's on my broccoli
My sweetcorn and my peas!

45

Shoes

Kaye Umansky,
illustrated by Penny Dann

Red shoes, blue shoes,
Which ones shall I choose shoes?

Green shoes, white shoes,
Got to choose the right shoes.

Yellow shoes, pink shoes,
Which ones do you think shoes?

Black shoes, brown shoes,
Funny spotty clown shoes.

Red shoes, blue shoes,
Which shoes would you choose?

Me!

Roger McGough, illustrated by Lauren Child

If I were big
I'd want to be sky

If I were little
I'd want to be small elephant

If I were muffin
I'd want to be chocolate

If I were ice-cream
I'd want to be strawberry

(or chocolate)

If I were drink
I'd want to be **fizzy**

If I were circus
I'd want to be **clown**

If I were summer fair
I'd want to be **bouncy castle**

If I were tree
I'd want to be **toffee apple**

If I were car
I'd want to be **DOUBLE-DECKER BUS**

If I were water
I'd want to be **sea**

If I were someone else
I'd want to be **ME!**

Along Came a Bedtime

Ian Whybrow, illustrated by Axel Scheffler

Splashing in the bath
Just my baby and me –
Along came a DUCK
That was cheeky as can be.
"Daddad!" said the baby meaning: "Wash my back!"
In jumped the duck and the duck went . . .

Quack!

Driving in the car
Just my baby and me
(Whoops, we nearly forgot the duck. Start again.)
Driving in the car
Just my baby, duck and me,
Along came a SHEEP
That was woolly as can be.
"Daddad!" said the baby meaning: "Are you going far?"
In jumped the sheep
and the sheep went . . .

Baaa!

Sitting up in bed
   Just my baby and me
      (Whoops, we nearly forgot the duck.
         Hey, and we nearly forgot the sheep. Start again.)
Sitting up in bed
Baby, ducky, sheep and me,
Along came a COW
Just as milky as can be.
"Daddad!" said the baby meaning: "Are you tired, too?"
In jumped the cow
and the cow went . . .

Mooo!

We read a little book
And we snuggled up tight.
"Daddad!" said the baby meaning: "Please turn out the light!"

52

The light went CLICK meaning: "Hush . . . not a peep!"
So we whispered

Mooo!

Baaa!

Quack!

Night-night!

Then everyone went to . . .

sleep.

Crumbly Castle

Nick Sharratt

Crumbly Castle was a dull,
boring grey.
It really couldn't stay
that way.

King Fred said, "Paint it Red!"

Queen Jean said, "Make it Green!"

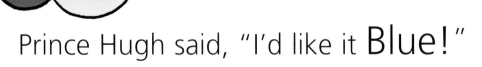

Prince Hugh said, "I'd like it Blue!"

Princess Louise said, "Yellow please!"

So they got paint and brushes and weren't they clever!

Now they live in the **stripiest** castle ever!

Bouncing!

Nick Butterworth

Bouncing, bouncing,
bouncing up and down.
Bouncing always makes me smile;
it's hard to bounce and frown.

Bouncing, bouncing,
bouncing high and low.
When I finish bouncing,
I'll have another go.

Bouncing, bouncing,
is such a lovely feeling.
Once, I bounced so high, my head
nearly touched the ceiling!

Bouncing, bouncing,
with a friend or two.
Actually, we're more than that
we're really . . . quite a few.

Bouncing, bouncing,
is fun for all of us.
We never bounce with shoes on.
(That is dangerous.)

Bouncing, bouncing,
my friends are out of puff.
I could bounce for ever,
but my friends have had enough.

Bouncing, bouncing,
twisting round and round.
I wonder why my tummy
makes that funny sound.

Bouncing, bouncing,
I'd better stop – and quick!
I had a glass of milk just now
and I'm feeling . . .

Busy, Busy Day
Alex Ayliffe

stretching

munching

crawling

exploring

one step . . .

two steps . . .

oops . . . bumping!

One Baby Bear!

John Prater

1 Baby Bear

took **2** big chairs,

3 coloured sheets,

and **4** cushion seats,

and made,

can you guess?

A bit of a mess . . .

So big Grandbear

took **4** cushion seats,

3 coloured sheets,

2 big chairs, and

1 Baby Bear,

and made,

guess again?

A wonderful snuggly den.

Nudey-Dudey

Helen Stephens

Nudey-dudey
splish, splash, splosh
rub-a-dub-dub
wash, wash, wash

Bathtime's over
pull out the plug
gurgle, gurgle, gurgle
glug, glug, glug

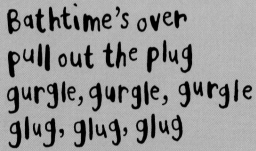

Nudey-dudey
drip, drop, drip
little wet footprints
jump, hop, skip

Ten drippy fingers
ten drippy toes
one squashy bum
one red nose

Nudey-dudey
tickle, tickle, tickle
warm and dry now
wiggle, wiggle, wiggle

Rub-a-dub-dub
ruffle buffle hair
fluffy, buffy, spikey
now we're nearly there

Nudey-dudey
bend your knees
into your pyjamas
legs up please

Weary sleepy
snuggle into bed
snoozy, droopy   Z Z Z ...

Apples and Pears

Vivian French, illustrated by Sue Heap

Apples and pears, apples and pears
Humpty Dumpty is falling down stairs!
Call the King's horses and all the King's men
Old King Cole is merry again

The Fiddlers Three begin to play
Over the Hills and Far Away
Tom, Tom the piper's son
Is counting plum stones, one by one

Jack jumps over his Christmas pie
And Georgie Porgie starts to cry
When the boys come out to play
The moon is shining bright as day

Up the ladder and down the wall
Jack and Jill are going to fall
Climb back up again, Jack and Jill
Little Bo-Peep is on the hill

Little Bo-Peep has lost her sheep
But Little Boy Blue is fast asleep
Wake him up and play a tune
The cows are jumping over the moon

The dog and the cat play fiddle-de-dee
Hush-a-bye baby up in the tree
Apples and pears, apples and pears . . .
Humpty Dumpty is falling down stairs . . .

Perky Little Penguins

Tony Mitton, illustrated by Eric Carle

Perky little penguins
sliding on the ice.
"Ooh," squeak the penguins.
"Isn't this nice!"

Perky little penguins
jumping in the sea.
"Ooh," squeak the penguins.
"That's the place to be!"

Perky little penguins,
aren't you getting chilly?
"No," squeak the penguins.
"Don't be silly!"

Sleepy Daddy!

Malorie Blackman, illustrated by Ken Wilson-Max

Wake up, Daddy.

"The sun is shining," said Lizzy.

"Zzzz-zzzz," Dad snored.

Wake up, Daddy.

"The birds are singing," said Lizzy.

"Bluub-zzzz! Bluub-zzzz!" Dad snored even louder.

Wake up, Daddy.

"I want to play," said Lizzy.

"Later," Dad grumbled and went back to sleep.

So Lizzy thought and thought.

Wake up, Daddy.

"There's a rocket in our garden," said Lizzy.

Wake up, Daddy.

"There's a rickety-rackety robot behind the door," said Lizzy.

Wake up, Daddy.

"There's an angry dinosaur at the window," said Lizzy.

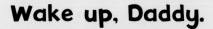

Daddy pulled the duvet up to his chin and went back to sleep.
So Lizzy thought and thought some more . . .

"I love you, Daddy," she whispered.

And Daddy opened his eyes
and stretched out his arms and said . . .

"I'm awake and it's cuddletime!"

Smile!

Jacqueline Wilson, illustrated by Posy Simmonds

Here is your mouth
Here is your nose
Here are your fingers
Here are your toes

Smile with your mouth
Wrinkle your nose
Wave all your fingers
When I tickle your toes!

A Cat on the Mat

Shirley Hughes

Scratch, scratch!
"What's that?"
"Oh look, Mum, it's a cat!
A little striped cat,
A cat on the mat!
Can we let him in?"

"Oh no, I'm afraid
we can't let him in.
He's not our little cat.
Go away, little cat!"

Miaow, miaow!
"What's that?"
"He's still there, Mum,
that little cat –
such a dear little cat!
Oh please can we let him in?"

"No, no, certainly not!
We can't let him in.
We don't want a cat.
We don't need a cat.
Shoo! Shoo!
Go away, little cat!"

Time to go out.
"Come along, here's your coat
and your warm woolly hat."
"Oh, Mum, look who's there!
It's the little striped cat!
Over there, by the gate –
Isn't he great?"

"Yes, a dear little cat.
But not *our* little cat.
We can't keep a cat.
Go home, little cat!"

"*Perhaps he hasn't got a home.
Perhaps he's all alone.
Can't he stay by the gate?*"

"Well, yes, I guess.
But he'll soon run off.
Off to his own place –
Run off now, there's a good cat!"

Home again.
And: *"Oh look, there's the cat!*
He's back on our mat!
Can we give him some milk?"

"Well, just a drop.
But he can't come inside.
When he's licked up his milk
he must go off.
Off you go, little cat!"

"Look, he's cleaning his whiskers!
He's having a wash
on our mat!
Such a dear little cat!"

"Yes, very dear.
But we really don't want . . .
We really don't need . . . "

Pitterpat!
"Listen to that!
It's raining outside.
Poor little cat!
He's still on the mat,
And he terribly, terribly wants to come in!"

"Oh well, I suppose
He'd better come in.
Just for a while, mind.
Just till he's dry . . .
He certainly is a nice little cat!"

"*Look, Mum,
now the cat's on the mat,
the mat by the fire!
Purring and purring
and washing his paws.
What a darling cat!*"

"Mmm . . . Yes, I guess
he *is* rather a darling cat . . . "

"*Now that little cat
is our little cat
and that's that!*"

Four Knowing Little Poe-ings

Michael Morpurgo, illustrated by Michael Foreman

Knowledge

I'd very much rather have knowledge
Than porridge,
Because porridge is horridge.

Everyone Knows

Everyone knows
That your nose is
A long, long way
From your toeses.
Which, if you
Think of it
Is just as it should be
Cos toeses, as you knowses,
Stink a bit.

Do You Know?

Do you know that
Without my hair
I'll soon be entirely bare up there?
It's a secret I share
Only with friends who care.

I Don't Know

I don't know why,
But getting older hurts my shoulder
And knobbles my knees
And hobbles my hips.
Yet older is wiser, I'm told.
Oh yeah! I'm telling you,
I hunger to be younger.

More! More! More!

Rose Impey, illustrated by Arthur Robins

Up and down.
And side to side.
Baby loves to ankle ride.

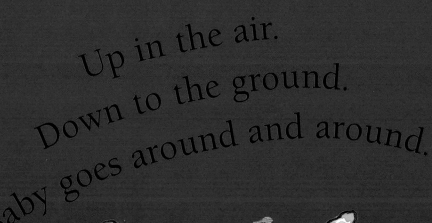

Up in the air.
Down to the ground.
Baby goes around and around.

Baby's riding
High and low.
Quick! Quick! Quick!
Then slow . . . slow . . . slow.

Up to the ceiling.
Down to the floor.
Baby loves it.
More! More! More!

Spiders Spin and Swallows Fly

Ruth and Ken Brown

Spiders spin
Worms wiggle
and bees buzz round and round.

Frogs jump
Slugs slide
and fish swim round and round.

Swans glide
Ducks dive
and swallows fly round and round –
They are off to a land, far away,
where it's sunny and warm,
not cold and grey.

Wriggle, Wriggle, Wriggle

Tony Mitton, illustrated by Sam Williams

Here's a little ladybird
coming in to land.
Cheeky little ladybird,
that's my hand!

Here's a little spider
spinning on a thread.
Hey, little spider,
that's my head!

Here's a little caterpillar
crawling on my toe.
Wriggle, wriggle, wriggle
ooh, you're tickling so!

Funny little creatures,
you don't belong on me.
Back into the grass you go,
one, two, three!

Dinnertime

Jane Simmons

One by one the animals come

And skip and hop and flip and run

Bleating and cheeping

A Potty Poem

David Melling

Georgina was a fussy child,
Her bright new potty drove her wild.
Poor Mummy said with some concern,
"But darling you must try and learn."
While bravely Daddy sat to show,
How clever children like to go!

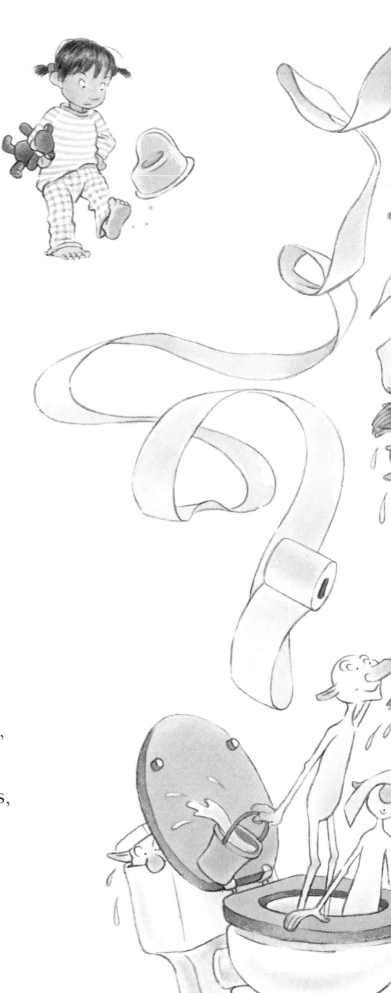

For months they tried, oh how she'd laugh,
(Now she's done it in the bath!)
Her parents groaned and blamed themselves,
"That's it! Let's call The Toilet Elves!"
Giggles gurgled in the plumbing,
Georgina said, "I think they're coming!"

The Elves sprang from the noisy loo,
Bowed low and said, "How do you do?"
With mop and bucket on the floor,
They swiftly turned and closed the door.
Muffled squeals that made you blush,
Were soon drowned out with one big flush.

And then . . .

The door swung silently ajar,
To show the strangest sight so far;
At last,
Their happy smiling daughter,
Doing what the Elves had taught her!

You Can See Them Too

Brian Patten,
illustrated by David Wojtowycz

I saw an elephant smuggling snowdrops
Through the jungle heat,
I saw a giraffe in a business suit
At the end of our street.

I saw an ocean freezing over,
I saw a river running dry,
I saw a somersaulting rabbit,
I saw a weasel blow his nose and cry.

I saw all these things today,
Honestly, it's true.
Just close your eyes and picture them,
And you can see them too.

The Splishy-Splashy Day

Philip Ardagh, illustrated by Russell Ayto

Today is a splishy-splashy day.
Little Pink Duck goes outside to play.
Her wellies are yellow and her raincoat is blue.
She jumps in the puddles.

Splash!

What a fun thing to do.

Pitter-patter, raindrops land on her beak,
Bounce off her green hat and run down her cheek!
She opens her brolly, with the funny frog eyes,
Twirls it around and looks up at the sky.
She stares in amazement and lets out a "Quack!"
She takes one step backwards . . .

Ooops!

. . . lands flat on her back!

Little Pink Duck is all in a muddle.
Her feathers are wet and she's **in a puddle!**
For up in the sky is a blob that's bright red.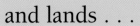
It's blowing towards her . . .

and lands . . .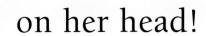

on her head!

It's a party balloon with a long piece of string.
Holding on tight is a wet furry **thing.**

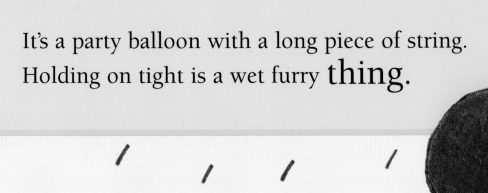

"Squeak!"

says the thing.
He's a tiny brown mouse.

He goes with Little Pink Duck . . .

to dry off at her house!

Bedtime

Berlie Doherty,
illustrated by Christian Birmingham

Your hand in my hand

Warm and tight

Climb up the stairs

And kiss goodnight

The Dreambirds

Jane Ray

What will the Dreambirds bring tonight?
What pictures to your head?
With feathered wings so colourful,
To your peaceful bed.

Will they bring you shadows, Love,
Or softly call your name?
Will they sing a silent song
Or play a secret game?

And when the morning comes at last
And you tumble into day
Will that silver dream be there
Or will it slip away?

Now let me rock you in my arms
And sing this lullaby
And let me tell you of my love
As you begin to fly.

AFTERWORD
Chris Meade, illustrated by Quentin Blake

THE REMARKABLE BOOKSTART PROJECT, initiated and run by Booktrust, came out of the realisation that children were arriving at school with no notion of how a book "worked". One day (actually in the early 1990s), Wendy Cooling, then Booktrust's Head of Children's Services, was visiting an infant school and began to notice the behaviour of the four- and five-year-old children there. She saw that they just weren't used to opening books and turning pages to enjoy the pictures and stories inside; in fact it was clear that some of them had never handled books before.

Wendy felt that something had to be done – so, how could Booktrust make sure that every child was introduced to books early in their lives? The idea dawned of putting a bag of books into the hands of new parents, and Bookstart was born. Here's how it works: by supplying free books for every family in the UK, given by health visitors at Baby's eight-month check, Bookstart gives all families the opportunity to enjoy the delight of sharing books with babies. The bag contains an invitation to join the library (a great haven for parents of small children), two board books, and a beautifully illustrated booklet on the benefits and pleasures of books for babies. It was a breathtakingly simple and effective idea.

Bookstart was first launched in Birmingham in 1992 with the help of Birmingham University, South Birmingham Health Authority, the Birmingham Library Service, and support from the Roald Dahl Foundation and the Unwin Charitable Trust. By 2000, thanks to funding from Sainsbury's plc, Bookstart was developed nationwide. Now it is funded by the government and supported by a range of children's book publishers.

Sharing a book with a baby is a great joy – and through rhymes, stories and pictures lots of learning takes place too. No wonder Bookstart babies have been shown to be ahead of their peers in literacy and numeracy as they grow up – still hungry for books even when they've grown out of chewing them! That's why this project is at the heart of Booktrust's aim – to encourage reading all through life.

Chris Meade

Chris Meade
Director, Booktrust
www.booktrust.org.uk